7639743

A Gift To: Taylor

Greening

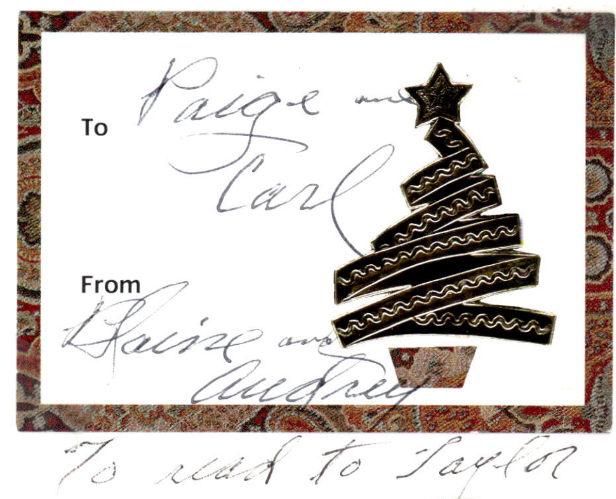

From:

Our Family Lines

325 E. 3450 N.
Provo, UT 84604

Printed in The United States of
America.

2 3 4 5 6 7 8 9 10 (Pbk)

Printers:
Publishers Press
Salt Lake City, UT

Distribution:
**Publishers Distribution Center,
Incorporated**
805 W. 1700 S.,
Salt Lake City , UT 84104

1-800-922-9681

ISBN 0-9648203-1-5 (Pbk)

What Do They Do All Day In Heaven?

By Staci Crowton Thomas

Illustrated By Helen Thomas

Our Family Lines

Foreword

A woman once said to me in response to my book <u>The Christmas Box</u>, " How could you understand so well the pain of losing a child? You must have lost a child yourself."

I said, "No, but I fear it so greatly I think I know what it feels like."

The woman somberly replied, "No, only those who have lost a child know what it feels like."

I humbly apologized. She was right. Only those who have been through the experience can truly understand. In the past two years I have had the poignant opportunity of meeting with hundreds of people who have lost children. I have come to recognize the signs of their grief and to feel, albeit in a very small way, their pain. What I rarely see are the children, and I worry about them.

I am pleased to recommend <u>What Do They Do All Day In Heaven?</u> as I believe it gives a parent and a child an opportunity to discuss the loss of a sibling and to examine their feelings instead of burying them with their loved one.

There is another reason I recommend this book. When I first met Staci and Helen Thomas, I was taken by their genuine passion for their book and their sense of personal mission to address the children who grieve. This book, like its author and illustrator, is motivated by love. And that is always the right place to start the healing process.

Richard Paul Evans
New York Times Best Selling Author, <u>The Christmas Box</u>

Preface

Losing a child breaks your heart, and although a broken heart can be mended, it is still missing pieces-sometimes very big pieces. Sometimes the most painful parts are the faces of your other children. You still see their potential. You still feel their joy, their eager anticipation, their smiles. Most of all you know what you have lost.

That dreadful morning that I found my little daughter is forever etched in my mind. But almost even more disturbing were the confused and frightened faces of my two-year-old twin girls who were right there with me. They didn't understand. It was beyond explaining why their new little sister was suddenly gone, why the paramedics came, why they took her away, and why her twin brother stayed. They simply did not understand.

As time went on, I watched as they created their own version of heaven. They created this simple, gentle, curious place. My husband and I found that we were much more comforted by their views than they were by ours. So we went with theirs.

Welcome to their heaven!

Author

<u>Staci Crowtron Thomas</u> has always been a writer. For as long as Staci can remember, she has constantly had a pen and paper within reach. Her poems and short stories come from her heart with inspiration from her children and life's experiences. As a professional woman and mother, she and her husband, Matt, keep their family as a central focus. Her decision to publish came from the realization that her work can comfort others.

Illustrator

<u>Helen Thomas</u> feels closer to heaven when showing love for children. Through her art she has found a means of affecting people not only on an artistic level, but emotionally and mentally. Helen is currently a Design Illustration major at Brigham Young University. Her goal is to continue illustrating books that will help children deal with their problems and bring joy into their lives.

This book is dedicated to my parents
Dave and Dallyne Crowton for believing
everything I ever did was brilliant.
I love you both.
— Staci

In loving memory of Bailey Jane Thomas,
Brandon Anderson, Kimball Mckay Dyer and all
the other children who play in Heaven.

What does my sister do
when she goes to heaven?

Does she laugh?
Does she cry?

Does she stay up past
eleven?

Does she get to have bangs
and very long hair?

Does she get to wear dresses
everyday over there?

Does she slide down the rainbows

and jump on the beds?

Does she sleep in the halo
she wears on her head?

Does she sleep on her
tummy because of her
wings?

Does she know that at Christmas
everyone sings?

Does she ever need Band-Aids?
Do they make her feel better?

Maybe in her spare time she
could write me a letter.

Does she ever get hic-cups?
Does she ever get sad?

Does she ever get really,
really, mad?

Does she get to eat lunch
or take a long rest?

Does she get nervous like me
when she takes a math test?

I'm curious, you know,
if heaven's okay,
if she fits in, if it's
as hard as first grade?

If she ever gets scared,
does she know where I am.

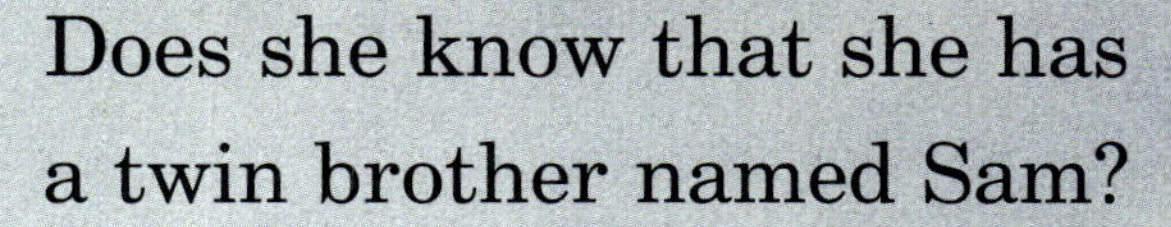

Does she know that she has
a twin brother named Sam?

Does she know

that her Christmas stocking still
hangs next to ours?

HERE

Does she know Grandma Helen,
does she sleep in her arms?

Does she crawl on her lap
and rock in a chair?

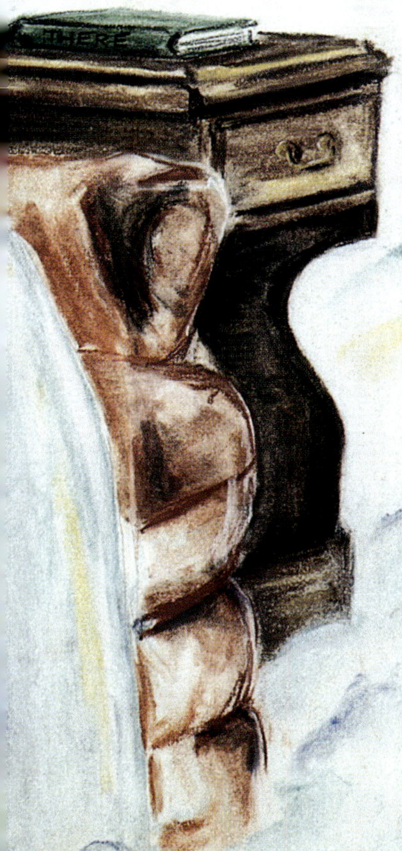

Do they read stories
about here
and
stories about
there?

Does she know that I miss her,
Does she know that I care?

Does she know that we have the
same color of hair?

Does she keep all the
balloons that go up to the skies?

Does she have the same
twinkle as mom's
in her eyes?

Do they sing lots of songs?
Does she know all the words?

Does she look up

or look down

to see all the birds?

Happy 7th
Birthday

Does she know that this summer I'll be
turning seven?